WALT DISNEY PRODUCTIONS
presents

The Aristocats

Random House ▥ New York

Library of Congress Cataloging in Publication Data
Disney (Walt) Productions.
Walt Disney Productions presents The aristocats.
(Disney's wonderful world of reading, no. 14)
A pampered cat and her three kittens find their way home after being abandoned by a villainous butler.
[1. Cats—Fiction] I. Title. II. Title: The aristocats. PZ7.D625Ar6 [E] 73-15626. ISBN 0-394-82553-5, ISBN 0-394-92553-X (lib. bdg.)

Duchess was a perfect cat.
She had soft, smooth fur
and bright, blue eyes.
When she walked,
she took little steps
and held up her tail in
just the right way.

Duchess had three kittens.
She was teaching them
to be perfect kittens.

Tu-Tu was learning
to paint.

Marie was learning
to sing.

Berly was learning to play the piano.

And they were all learning to hold up
their tails in just the right way.

Duchess and her kittens lived with a very
rich old lady named Madame.

Madame was very good to her cats.

She gave them the softest pillows and
the thickest cream and the prettiest bows.

Madame had a butler named Edgar.
Edgar hated cats.
He hated fluffing their pillows and
fixing their cream and tying their bows.

Every day Edgar muttered to himself,
"These cats have got to go!"

One night Edgar put something extra in the cream—sleeping pills!

Then he took the little bowls of cream to Duchess and her kittens.

"Do not forget your manners," said Duchess.

"Thank you, Edgar," said Marie, Tu-Tu, and Berly.

Duchess and the kittens
lapped up the cream.

It was delicious!
But soon Duchess felt very sleepy.
Her eyelids began to droop.
Berly and Marie were yawning.
Tu-Tu was already asleep.

When all the cats were asleep,
Edgar put them in their basket.

Late that night he carried the basket
out to his motorcycle.

He took the cats for a long ride.

When he was far
away from the city,
he left the basket
under a bridge.

"Now they will never
find their way back,"
thought Edgar.

In the morning Duchess and the kittens
woke up.

Everything looked strange.

"Where are we, Mama?" asked Tu-Tu.

"Do not be afraid, dear," said Duchess.

"I will think of a way to get home."

But Duchess did not know what to do.

Just then she saw another cat.
"Hi!" called the cat.
"I'm Tom O'Malley, the alley cat."
Duchess could see that he
was an alley cat.
He held his tail all wrong.

"Mr. O'Malley," said Duchess.
"Can you tell me the way to the city?"
"Tell you, fair lady?" said O'Malley.
"I will take you there on my magic carpet."

When the kittens heard
this, they leaped out
of the basket.
"Do you really have
a magic carpet?" asked Marie

"Kittens!" cried O'Malley.
"I didn't know you had kittens.
I was thinking of a magic carpet for two."

"Come along, children," said Duchess.
"Mr. O'Malley cannot help us."
And Duchess and her kittens walked away.

"Wait!" called O'Malley.
"I see my magic carpet
coming down the road."
O'Malley's magic carpet
looked like an old milk truck
on its way to the city.

O'Malley landed on the milk truck.
He hissed and howled.
"Help!" screamed the driver.
The truck screeched to a stop
and the driver got out.

"Where is that stupid cat?"
muttered the driver.

He did not see who was
climbing onto his truck.

So he got back in and
drove on down the road.

"Is anyone ready for breakfast?" said O'Malley.
"Where is it?" asked Tu-Tu.
"Just close your eyes and wiggle your noses,"
said O'Malley. "I need a little magic for this."
So the kittens closed their eyes and
wiggled their noses.

O'Malley uncovered a milk can.
"The magic worked," said O'Malley.
"Open your eyes and see."

The kittens opened their eyes.
"Milk!" cried Marie.
"O'Malley is terrific!"
"How true!" said O'Malley.

After a while,
the driver turned around.
"Jumping jailfish!"
he cried. "CATS!"

He stopped the truck and chased them away.

"What an awful man!" said Duchess.
"Now we will not get to the city."
"Stick with me, Duchess," said O'Malley.
"I know the way."

"O'Malley is so smart," said Marie.
'O'Malley is so brave," said Tu-Tu.
"When I grow up," said Berly,
"I am going to be just like O'Malley."

They came to some train tracks.
The tracks went over a river.
The kittens pretended to be a train.
"Whoo-whoo," cried Berly.
"Clickety-clack, clickety-clack,"
said Tu-Tu and Marie.

Suddenly they heard a real train coming.
It was right behind them.

O'Malley got everyone under the tracks
just in time.

The train whizzed by over their heads.

Marie was so scared,
she let go and fell off
the bridge.

"Help!" cried Marie.

O'Malley did
a daring dive.

He pulled Marie out of the river.
"How can I ever thank you?" asked Duchess.
"It's nothing," said O'Malley.
After that, the cats walked along the road.

At last they reached the city,
but it was very late.
"We will have to spend the night
with my friends," said O'Malley.

They climbed up to a roof
and looked in a window.

O'Malley's friends were
having a party.

"Hey! O'Malley is back,"
cried Scat Cat.

Everyone had fun.
Scat Cat sang a song.
It went like this:
  "Rinky Tinky,
  Think of that!
  To be a cat
  Without a hat!"

"Sing it, Scat!" said O'Malley.
"Yeah, sing it, Scat,"
said Berly and Marie.

Duchess and
O'Malley danced
all the dances
O'Malley knew.

After the party was over,
O'Malley and Duchess sat on the roof.
"You have been very kind to us,"
said Duchess. "We will miss you, but
tomorrow we must go back to Madame."

The kittens were watching
from the window.

"I don't want to go back," said Berly.
"I want to stay with O'Malley."

But the next morning, they went back
to Madame's house.

O'Malley waved good-by.

Edgar let the cats in.

He was not happy to see
them come back.

Edgar put
the cats
in a bag.

He put the bag in a trunk.
Then he called a moving van
to take the trunk far, far away.

DELIVER TO
TIMBUKTU
DO NOT RETURN!

Edgar carried the trunk out to the street.
The van was waiting.

O'Malley heard Duchess and the kittens
mewing inside.

O'Malley leaped at Edgar.
He hissed and howled.

Madame heard the howling.

She rushed outside to see what was going on.

There were Duchess and her kittens.

"Oh, my dearest Duchess," cried Madame.

"You are all safe."

Madame saw that Edgar was trying
to get rid of her cats.

"You are fired!" said Madame.

Edgar went away and never came back.

Madame said she needed a cat who was smart and brave.

So O'Malley decided to stay.

He was a very good father.

"How did we ever get along without you?" asked Duchess.

O'Malley just smiled.